POTLATCH
A Tsimshian Celebration

Library of Congress Cataloging-in-Publication Data
Hoyt-Goldsmith, Diane
   Potlatch: a Tsimshian celebration / by Diane Hoyt-Goldsmith:
photographs by Lawrence Migdale. - 1st ed.
         p.   cm.
   Summary: Describes the traditions of the Tsimshian Indians living in Metlakatla, Alaska, and in particular,
those connected with a potlatch they hold to celebrate their heritage.
   ISBN 0-8234-1290-3 (library)
 1. Potlatch - Alaska - Metlakatla - Juvenile literature.
 2. Tsimshian Indians - Rites and ceremonies - Juvenile literature.
 3. Tsimshian Indians - Social life and customs - Juvenile literature.
 4. Metlakatla (Alaska) - Social life and customs - Juvenile literature. [1. Potlatch. 2. Tsimshian Indians - Social
life and customs. 3. Indians of North America - Northwest, Pacific - Social life and customs.] I. Migdale,
Lawrence, ill. II. Title.
E99.T8H67   1997   96-41367
394.2'089974-dc20   CIP
                                                                                                AC

Acknowledgments
   We would like to thank David A. Boxley and his son David R. Boxley, for hosting us during the potlatch celebration in Metlakatla, Alaska, in September of 1994. We are honored to have been invited to document this
important occasion and have come away with many wonderful memories and new friendships.
   There are many individuals in the community who deserve a special word of thanks for their efforts and
cooperation: Floyd Guthrie, Master of Ceremonies for the potlatch; Wayne Hewson, totem pole carver and
member of the Killerwhale clan; Bill Holm; Bob Leask; Mique'l Aksren and the other members of the Git-Lak-Lik-
Staa dance group; Sissy Guthrie and Barbara Fawcett; Theo, Jerry, and Marcella McIntyre; the Fourth Generation
Dancers; and all the people in the Eagle, Raven, Killerwhale, and Wolf clans who made us feel welcome and
shared with us this wonderful event. Thanks also to Evelyn Vanderhoop and her children, Tiffany and David,
and to her mother, Delores Churchill, who introduced us to the Raven's Tail weaving traditions of the Northwest
Coast people.
   The cover illustrations for this book by David R. Boxley, show that he has already learned a great deal
about his Tsimshian culture and traditions. We are pleased to include the work of this talented young artist in
our book.

POTLATCH
A Tsimshian Celebration

by Diane Hoyt-Goldsmith
Photographs by Lawrence Migdale

Holiday House — New York

This book
is dedicated
to all the children of
Metlakatla, Alaska,
with the hope that
they will celebrate their
Tsimshian heritage
for many years to come.

David wears special ceremonial clothing called regalia (reh-GAY-lee-ah) for the potlatch.

My name is David. I am thirteen years old and spending the summer at my father's boyhood home in Metlakatla (met-lah-KAT-lah), Alaska. My people are the Tsimshians (TSIM-shee-ans), a tribe of Northwest Coast Indians. We are holding a potlatch to honor our heritage and celebrate our traditions.

The Tsimshians

David and his friend Tiffany weave strands of cedar bark together to make headbands. David will give the headbands away as gifts during the potlatch.

My people, the Tsimshians, are one of the tribes of the Northwest Coast Indians who have lived along the coastline of what is now the northwestern United States and British Columbia in Canada for many thousands of years. Although each tribe has its own language and customs, we share many traditions.

Living in small villages along the rivers, bays, and inlets of their rain forest home, the Indians of the Northwest Coast have survived and flourished. Salmon was a favorite food, always plentiful in the rivers. The people took their large canoes out on the ocean to fish for halibut and hunt for sea mammals. My ancestors ate shellfish that they found in the bays near their homes and hunted for game animals in the forests.

The dense rain forests were filled with evergreen trees called cedars. The wood from these trees provided strong planks for my ancestors to use in building their homes. They carved the cedar wood into bowls and storage boxes and made utensils for cooking and eating. The bark was pounded into soft fibers that were woven into warm blankets and clothing.

The Indians of the Northwest Coast were fortunate to live in a temperate climate. The summers were cool and rainy, and the winters mild. They spent the summer months collecting and preserving food. Then, during the winter, there was time for feasts and celebrations. People carved cedar logs into totem poles. They created beautiful cedar masks of animal spirits and used them to act out their legends and myths at the potlatches they held.

Long ago my ancestors had a society based upon clans, which are large, extended families. We believe that spiritual beings, in the form of birds and animals, are our ancient ancestors and the origin of our clans. Today in Metlakatla, we have four different clans — the Ravens, the Killerwhales, the Wolves, and the Eagles. I belong to the Eagle clan.

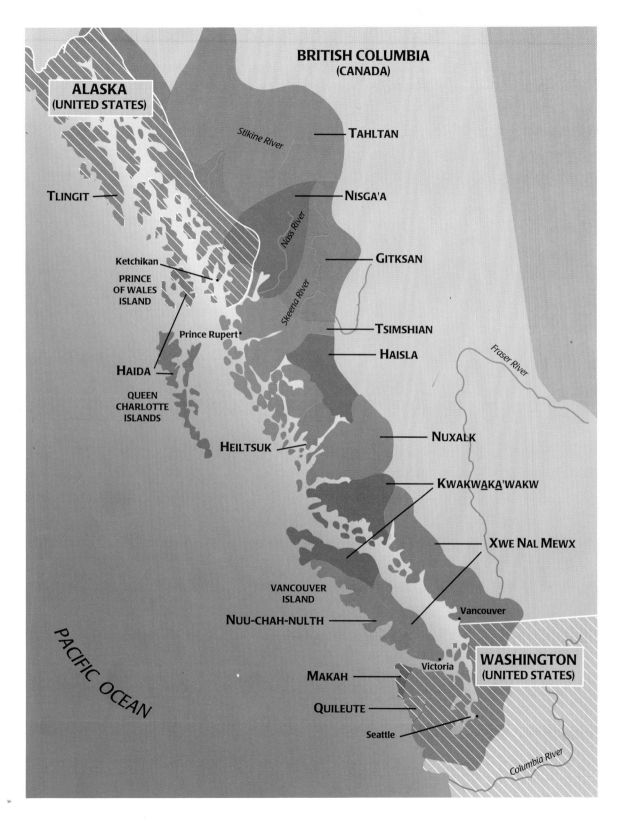

BRITISH COLUMBIA
(CANADA)

ALASKA
(UNITED STATES)

Stikine River

TAHLTAN

TLINGIT

NISGA'A

Nass River

Ketchikan
PRINCE
OF WALES
ISLAND

GITKSAN

Skeena River

Prince Rupert

TSIMSHIAN

HAISLA

Fraser River

HAIDA

QUEEN
CHARLOTTE
ISLANDS

HEILTSUK

NUXALK

KWAKWA̲KA̲'WAKW

XWE NAL MEWX

VANCOUVER
ISLAND

Vancouver

NUU-CHAH-NULTH

WASHINGTON
(UNITED STATES)

Victoria

MAKAH

QUILEUTE

Seattle

PACIFIC OCEAN

Columbia River

The Native Americans of the Northwest Coast

Tlingit

Tahltan

Nisga'a

Gitksan

Tsimshian

Haida

Haisla

Heiltsuk

Nuxalk

Kwakwa̲ka̲'wakw

Nuu-chah-nulth

Xwe Nal Mewx

Makah

Quileute

The people of the Northwest Coast still live along the shoreline of Washington and southern Alaska in the United States and British Columbia in Canada.

A History of the Potlatch

The Tsimshians and other Northwest Coast Indians have held potlatches for many hundreds of years. The potlatch served many important functions. Long ago, before my people had written deeds to show ownership of property and wills to prove inheritance, the potlatch was a way for people to claim rank and privileges.

The host of the potlatch would call all the people from nearby villages to come and stay for many days. A large feast would be prepared for the guests. Then, in front of the crowd, the host of the potlatch would claim a hereditary rank or privilege such as the name of a relative who had died or a position of leadership that lay vacant. By witnessing the event, the guests made the host's claim valid. In return, the host gave a valuable gift to each guest.

The potlatch was also a way people could learn about and witness major events in their cultural life. They might recognize a new chief, learn of a new name, or witness an adoption. The potlatch was an occasion for raising totem poles to express grief at the death of an important person and to honor that person's memory.

Potlatching served important social functions too. It was one of the few opportunities people had to gather in a large group. My ancestors enjoyed the potlatch because they could meet new people, be reunited with members of their clan, and hear the news from other villages. The potlatch was a time for my people to enjoy their culture. They listened to stories and songs and performed dances and dramas. A potlatch helped keep their legends and their history alive.

The giving of extravagant gifts during a potlatch was an important part of the tradition. The need for valuable gifts encouraged the arts among the Northwest Coast people to flourish. Intricate carvings on rattles, boxes, and headdresses made these objects desirable. Finely woven leggings, blankets, and dance aprons also made good gifts.

Tiffany's mother and grandmother are both well known for their weaving skills. Tiffany and her brother watch their grandmother as she creates a Raven's Tail design.

8

Hundreds of white mother-of-pearl buttons are sewn on the back of this button blanket to make a design.

David's father works hard for many months to make the gifts and the new regalia necessary for a large potlatch. He paints a drum as his friend Evelyn finishes sewing a button blanket.

Friends from all over the Northwest come to help David's father finish the potlatch gifts.

Each time a potlatch was held, the host would try to outdo all the others in the quantity and quality of gifts that were given away. Often a person would scrimp and save for years to afford the gifts for a potlatch. For this reason, only powerful, wealthy people were able to host a potlatch and holding a successful potlatch raised the social status of the host.

Potlatching was an important part of our culture until the first Europeans came to the Northwest Coast. Then things began to change. Sailing ships brought traders from Russia, France, and England to our shores with wool blankets, beads, buttons, metal tools, and guns. The ships returned home filled with fish and furs.

The Northwest Coast Indians made the blankets into warm, beautiful robes. On the back of the robes, they created images of animals outlined in hundreds of white buttons called crests. These images represented the clans. These button blankets, became an important part of a person's regalia. Undecorated blankets were a popular potlatch gift. Sometimes many hundreds were given away during a single potlatch.

The traders were soon followed by missionaries, who came to live among the Northwest Coast people and teach them about Christianity. To many of the European settlers, the potlatch tradition seemed strange. Giving away all of one's wealth did not seem right, especially during times when the people had very little. In 1885, the government of Canada passed a law that made holding a potlatch illegal.

Although the Northwest Coast people knew they could be arrested and sent to prison for participating in a potlatch, a small number continued to hold on to the tradition. Sometimes potlatches were held in secret. Other times people tried to go around the law by substituting large amounts of food for the elaborate handmade gifts they would normally give away. Sacks of flour and barrels of *ooligan* (OOH-leh-gan) grease, a tasty flavoring made from fermented fish, were given instead.

Some potlatch hosts tried a different approach. They went from door-to-door in the villages, delivering the potlatch gifts directly to the homes of their guests. In this way, they could avoid gathering in a large group and escape the attention of the authorities.

For many reasons, the potlatch tradition nearly disappeared among the Indians of the Northwest Coast. First of all, the law against potlatching discouraged many people from holding them. Other people were influenced by the missionaries who lived in their communities. They learned to think that the potlatch was wrong. As more settlers moved into the Northwest, the influence of European culture grew and native traditions began to fade. All of these reasons help to explain why the Tsimshians in Metlakatla did not hold a single potlatch for almost a hundred years.

This photograph, taken in 1898, shows a Tsimshian potlatch held in the village of Kispiox. A large stack of flour sacks can be seen in the center of the crowd. The flour will be given away to the potlatch guests.

A New Tsimshian Settlement

The first settlers to come to Annette Island were a group of 800 Tsimshians who followed a missionary named William Duncan in 1887. They came from Old Metlakatla, a Tsimshian village in British Columbia, with plans to build an ideal community. For Duncan, this meant a place where people would live according to Christian values. With Duncan's help, the Tsimshians built a lumber mill and a fish cannery. On Annette Island, in a new town they named Metlakatla, my ancestors had a good life, living off the bounty of nature.

Today most members of the Tsimshian tribe still live in British Columbia, Canada, in towns such as Port Simpson, Old Metlakatla, and Prince Rupert.

At low tide, David and his friends search for crabs hiding in the seaweed.

Metlakatla, Alaska

Today, Metlakatla, which means "inlet of the open sea" in the Tsimshian language, has a population of about 1,200 people. Located fifteen miles south of Ketchikan, Alaska, it is the only town on Annette Island. Nestled among mountain peaks and forests, Metlakatla can only be reached by boat, ferry, or seaplane.

A seaplane lands in Metlakatla's harbor.

Revival of the Potlatch

When my ancestors followed William Duncan to Annette Island, they became isolated from the rest of the Tsimshian people and from their ancient traditions and culture. Four generations passed, and no potlatches were held in Metlakatla. Christian traditions had replaced my ancestors' native ways.

Then, when I was just a little boy, my father helped organize the very first potlatch to be held since the Tsimshians came to Metlakatla. That first potlatch, given in honor of my great-grandmother after she died, created a new interest in our culture. People in Metlakatla began to realize what they had lost. New dance groups were formed. People who didn't have regalia started to make and collect it. Metlakatla, a town that had turned away from its roots, saw native traditions begin to flourish again.

David stands with his friends who are members of the children's dance group of Metlakatla. Called *Git-Lak-Lik-Staa*, which means "people of the island" in the Tsimshian language, the group performs for events like the potlatch.

The potlatch we are holding today began with my great-grandfather, Albert Bolton. All through his childhood, my father was close to his grandfather. Albert taught my father to speak the Tsimshian language and encouraged him to learn about their native culture and traditions. My father tells me that he learned life's most important lessons from his grandfather.

My father started thinking about holding another potlatch in Metlakatla to honor my great-grandfather on his 100th birthday. Although Albert died in 1992 at the age of ninety-eight, my father didn't give up on the idea of the potlatch. He decided to go ahead with his plans, but to make the potlatch a memorial instead.

David and his father visit Albert Bolton's grave. As they weed, David hears stories about his great-grandfather and about his father's experiences growing up in Metlakatla.

15

David's father makes his living as an artist, carving masks and totem poles in the traditional Tsimshian style. When he decided to hold the potlatch, he began by asking a group of friends and community leaders to help him. As they discussed how the potlatch should be organized, they worked together, carving spoons by hand from blocks of wood. As their ancestors did long ago, David's father and his friends carved more than a hundred spoons during these discussions — all to be given away as gifts at the potlatch.

A Potlatch Feast

As in days of old, our potlatch begins with a feast. Since the potlatch in Metlakatla involves the entire community, my father and the other planners decided that it should last four nights. Then each night of the potlatch could be hosted by a different clan. Providing food is a way clan members traditionally welcome their guests and make them feel at home.

Everyone in Metlakatla is invited to come to the potlatch. In addition, relatives and visiting dance groups from other Northwest Coast tribes make the numbers of guests swell even more. My father and I estimate that there will be more than a thousand people who will sit down each night to eat dinner at the feast.

Each of the four clans will serve a different menu. The Raven clan will start things off on the first night with a meal of fresh, broiled salmon. Next, the Wolf clan will provide the crowd with a halibut feast. The Killerwhale clan will serve venison, and on the last night, the Eagles will cook a meal featuring only native foods — herring eggs, seaweed, and a local favorite — a fish called *ooligans*, served both smoked and fried.

(Top) Floyd Guthrie, the Master of Ceremonies for the potlatch, greets the guests as they arrive.

(Left) The people of Metlakatla enjoy a feast of native foods.

Raising Potlatch Poles

On the first day of the potlatch, I am in charge of raising a small totem pole. I give directions as a group of my friends carry the pole to the place where I want it to stand. They push it up in front of the house where my father grew up. We bury the bottom part of the totem pole in the ground. Although I am nervous, I know just what to do because I have helped my father raise totem poles before. When the pole is standing straight, I feel proud.

The pole is dedicated to my mother's father, Sherwood, who died last year. He was an important person in my life. I remember all the times we spent together on camping trips and the wonderful handmade toys he gave me when I was a little boy. I'm glad to have this pole to remember him by.

David, dressed in regalia, directs the raising of a totem pole. A group of Tsimshian children from Metlakatla help carry and raise the pole.

After the pole raising, David dances to celebrate. The other children join in by singing and playing drums.

As a gift for all those who help me raise the pole, I made a silk-screen print that shows a salmon leaping. I made hundreds of copies so I could give one to every person who would come to watch the pole raising. By witnessing the event, they make what we do valid and memorable.

(Top) David's print is a gift for all those who help raise the pole and for all those who watch.

(Bottom) The totem pole, called "The Salmon Fisherman," shows a man riding on a salmon.

19

One of my father's friends, Wayne Hewson, worked all summer carving his very first totem pole. Although he has worked as a carver's apprentice helping my father with several other poles, this is the first time he has made a pole all by himself. He decided to take on this challenge because he knew the potlatch would be a good time to carve a pole for the community in honor of his clan, the Killerwhales.

The day after the children help me raise my pole, a group of people from the Killerwhale clan help Wayne put his pole up in front of the Senior Center in Metlakatla. The pole Wayne made shows the figure of a bear on the bottom and a killerwhale, with a tall dorsal fin, at the top. Rather than stand as a memorial to a person, Wayne's pole represents the entire Killerwhale clan.

Just a few days before the potlatch begins, Wayne Hewson puts the finishing touches on his first totem pole.

(Top) Volunteers carry the Killerwhale pole in a procession led by people in regalia, singing and playing the drums.

(Left) Standing proudly in front of the completed pole, Wayne Hewson dedicates the pole in honor of the people of the Killerwhale clan in Metlakatla, Alaska.

Raising a Memorial Pole

On the last day of the potlatch, another new pole is raised. Carved by David's father, the pole is a gift to the people of Metlakatla. In the traditional manner, the pole is carried by hand to the place where it will be raised. Then, the pole is pulled up with ropes. Finally it stands tall against the sky. David's father tells the crowd of his gratitude toward his grandfather Albert Bolton and his pride on this day. The pole, called "Eagle and Rainbow" symbolizes the cultural rebirth of Metlakatla. The rainbow represents hope for the future.

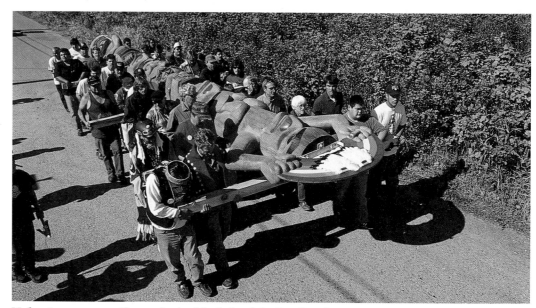

Volunteers carry the pole to Metlakatla's Senior Center.

Working together, the people pull the pole upright with ropes.

Once in position, the people make sure the pole is secure.

David's father dedicates the pole to the memory of his grandfather Albert Bolton.

Dedications and New Names

On each night of the potlatch, many new button blankets are dedicated. Before a new piece of regalia can be worn, we like to present it to the public at a potlatch. A dedication takes place in this way. A new blanket is brought out in front of the crowd. It is displayed, and the name of its maker is announced to everyone. The crowd is told for whom the blanket was made and to whom it is dedicated. Afterward, the blanket can be worn by its owner to any ceremony. On the four nights of the potlatch, more than sixty new blankets, each one a beautiful work of art, are presented and dedicated.

David's father dedicates a new button blanket during the potlatch. On the back is the design of an eagle and rainbow, created out of buttons and beads. The blanket was made for David's father by his friend Evelyn. The edges are woven in the Raven's Tail design.

Our potlatch is also an occasion for adopting new members into the clans and a time for giving new names. Among the Tsimshian, an Indian name is very important. We consider a name to be a possession, something of value that we own. My friend Mique'l (my-kee-EL) receives the name *shgu-goad lax shgeeg*. The name means "devoted eagle" in the Tsimshian language. It was given to her by the leaders of the children's dance group because of her hard work and dependability.

There are many reasons for special adoptions among our people. Some children, like me, have a father who is Tsimshian and a mother who is non-Indian. The rules of clan membership say a person belongs to his or her mother's clan. If the mother does not have a clan, neither does the child. I am a member of the Eagle clan only because my mother was adopted by the Eagles at the first potlatch held in Metlakatla when I was a little boy.

(Left) Mique'l, standing in the middle, receives a new name at the potlatch.

(Right) Theo McIntyre adopts her nephew into the Raven clan. After his adoption, he can wear the Raven crest on his regalia.

Dancing at the Potlatch

Everything that happens at a potlatch is important. I like to witness the dedications, the adoptions, and the giving of names, but I am happy there is time for fun, too. Playing drums and singing at the top of their voices, the different dance groups bring a feeling of celebration to the potlatch.

Some dances are very old and have come down to us from long ago. Metlakatla's adult dance group, the Fourth Generation Dancers, performs a dance at the potlatch that had been given away long ago to another tribe, the Tlingits, in payment of a debt. The Tlingits gave the dance back to the Tsimshians so it could be danced for this potlatch. Some new dances and songs were created especially for this potlatch. Like our Indian names, we consider songs, dances, and dramas as valuable possessions, to be collected and cherished from one generation to the next.

One kind of entertainment that we all enjoy is a Nax Nox story. *Nax Nox* is a term for the Tsimshian "Spirit Helper." In the old days, Tsimshians would seek a Nax Nox in nature. It might be an animal or a bird, and in times of need, a Tsimshian could call upon the Nax Nox for help.

During the potlatch, there are several presentations of Nax Nox stories. Using masks and pantomime, dancers act out the tale. One of these is a story and song that my father wrote for his friend Theo about a crab and a cockle, a shellfish that we love to eat.

Theo's daughter, Marcella, dances the part of the cockle, wearing a mask that my father carved. It has a little sprayer hidden under the mask. At a certain moment in the song, she dances up to her mother and squirts her with water. She acts just like a real cockle — they always squirt water at you when you try to dig them from the sand. Everyone laughs and laughs. Even though she is a little wet afterward, Theo likes her new song, too. The song and story are now her possessions, to sing and perform at other potlatch celebrations.

For many young people in Metlakatla, this potlatch is their first opportunity to participate in this ancient tradition.

(Top) **Git-Lak-Lik-Staa**, the children's dance group of Metlakatla, performs for the potlatch guests.

(Left) At the beginning of the potlatch, all the clans participate in the Grand Entry. For this dance, a crowd of people in regalia fills the gymnasium.

Potlatch Gifts

The giving of gifts is still one of most important parts of the potlatch. Every person who attends receives one. Some gifts are handmade works of art like the wooden spoons and the hand-painted drums that my father and his friends made. Food is another kind of gift presented to guests at a potlatch. Jars of *ooligan* oil, a native delicacy, are welcomed by the people in Metlakatla. Wild berries are made into jellies or baked into pies. Skilled artists from the community create artwork and posters to distribute during the potlatch. There are also commemorative mugs, notepads, and handcrafted items such as beaded leather purses. Practical gifts such as blankets, boxes of apples, and sets of cooking pots are also given away.

In ancient times, the distribution of gifts at a potlatch followed strict rules. The most important guests were given the biggest and the best gifts. Today, our most important guests are the elders of our community. They get seats in the front row and are given their gifts first. In this way, we honor them.

Each night during the potlatch, after the dedications and adoptions are finished, the clan hosting the potlatch calls for a Ad'm Nak (AH-dum NUKSH) payment. Everyone at the potlatch whose father belongs to the host clan puts money into a large collection box. It can be any amount, but usually people give one-dollar bills. Then everyone whose wife or husband belongs to the host clan puts a contribution into the box. Finally, all those with a mother belonging to the host clan adds to the collection.

After the money is collected and counted, it is redistributed to all the people at the potlatch who are not members of the clan making the payment. Each night, a different clan makes the payment and distributes the proceeds in a similar manner. By making the Ad'm Nak payments, we believe that a person honors his or her ancestors.

A member of the Raven clan deposits Ad'm Nak payments into a bentwood box.

The Wolf clan commissioned David's father to make this silk-screen print to give away at the potlatch.

(Left) Elders, honored with seats in the front row, receive their gifts first at a potlatch. Members of the Killerwhale clan distribute hand-sewn items and canned salmon.

(Below) The Eagle clan gathers to give away homemade jellies and pies and boxes of fruit.

When the potlatch is over, I stand next to my father, proud that his leadership and talents have made this potlatch a reality. I realize how lucky I am to have been a part of this important traditional event.

I am happy because this potlatch has given all the men, women, and children in this small island town a chance to stand up and show the world that they are proud of their culture. During the potlatch, many people I know were dancing with their clan and wearing regalia for the first time in their lives.

For four days, we wore our crests and regalia. We sang many old songs and some new ones. We danced, we honored our ancestors, and we all experienced a new pride in our identity. The Tsimshian culture and traditions, lost to us for a time, are now alive and well in Metlakatla.

David and his father are proud that the potlatch is a success.

30

GLOSSARY

Ad'm Nak (AH-dum NUKSH) A Tsimshian term for the collection and distribution of money by the clans in honor of their ancestors during a potlatch celebration.

button blanket A ceremonial cape made from a wool blanket and decorated with crests outlined in hundreds of white mother-of-pearl buttons.

clan A family group with common ancestors who, according to tradition, have descended from mythical animal spirits.

cockle An edible shellfish with two heart-shaped shells that is found along the shores in the Pacific Northwest.

crest Symbolic representations of animals that identify the clans of the Northwest Coast people. Used on houses, button blankets, canoes, grave markers, and many other objects to show clan ownership.

Git-Lak-Lik-Staa means "people of the island" in the Tsimshian language and is the name of Metlakatla's children's dance group.

Long House A large building constructed of cedar logs and planks, used by the Tsimshians for their public meetings and ceremonies.

Metlakatla (met-lah-KAT-lah) The only town on Annette Island, settled by the Tsimshians who followed a missionary named William Duncan in 1885.

mother-of-pearl The pearl-like coating on the inside of certain seashells.

Nax Nox A Tsimshian "Spirit Helper," usually in the form of an animal or bird, who can help a person in times of need.

ooligan (OOH-leh-gan) A term for a small, oily fish (eulochon) that is eaten by the Tsimshian people and used as a flavoring for other foods.

potlatch An important ceremony for the people of the Northwest Coast in which adoptions, regalia dedications, namings, and memorials are publicly witnessed.

Raven's Tail A style of weaving by the people of the Northwest Coast in which the soft hairs of a mountain goat are made into beautiful, geometric patterns.

regalia (reh-GAY-lee-ah) Ceremonial clothing worn by the people of the Northwest Coast for special occasions, including button blankets, frontlets, masks, leggings, aprons, and other articles, usually decorated with the owner's crest.

totem poles A tall, carved monument made from the trunk of a cedar tree which portrays animal and human figures and is made as a memorial to a person who has died or to commemorate an event.

Tsimshian (TSIM-shee-an) A tribe of Northwest Coast Indians who live in British Columbia and on Annette Island in Alaska.

INDEX

Page numbers in italic type indicate photographs.

Metlakatla's adult dance group, the Fourth Generation Dancers, perform in front of the Long House. They take their name from the fact that it was four generations from the time the Tsimshians came to Annette Island until they began to revive their traditional culture.